CRAZY
ANIMAL
STORIES

By Anne-Marie Dalmais

Translated by Evelyn Scott

Illustrated by Genji

McGRAW-HILL BOOK COMPANY
New York   St.Louis   San Francisco

First published in the United States of America 1982
by McGraw-Hill Book Company.

ISBN 0-07-015198-9
Library of Congress Cataloging in Publication Data
Dalmais, Anne Marie.
    Crazy animal stories.
    Summary: Episodes in prose and verse feature a good-
natured giraffe, a baboon prankster, a shaggy yak, and
other animal friends.
    [1. Animals—Fiction. 2. Animals—Poetry]
I. Genji, ill. II. Title.
PZ7.D166Cr 1982   [E]   82-10083
ISBN 0-07-015198-9

Printed in Spain by Imprenta Juvenil, S. A. - Lappas - Barcelona

CONTENTS

MISS GIRAFFE'S FLOWERED PAJAMAS

Miss Giraffe came back from the city carrying a large box and smiling with all her spots.

"What's inside the box? What did you buy?" all her neighbors demanded, bursting with curiosity.

"You'll find out!" said Miss Giraffe, keeping her eyes half closed so she would look more mysterious.

All the neighbors gathered in a circle around her, shoving a little as they tried to see and squealing with excitement. In the crowd there were some chimpanzees, an ostrich, several parrots, three gazelles, a zebra, and even Mrs. Chameleon, who had come out for a little walk while her five babies were asleep.

Miss Giraffe untied the striped ribbon, wound it carefully on one hoof, and set it in the grass nearby. Then, still taking her time, she lifted the lid from the box and placed it beside the ribbon.

"Quick! Quick!" the gazelles begged her, feeling that they could not last another second without knowing what was in the box.

"Please do hurry!" cried a chimpanzee, all on edge because Miss Giraffe unpacked so slowly.

Miss Giraffe frowned. "If this bothers you so much," she said, "I'll close the box up again."

"No, no!" her neighbors cried from every side. "We really don't mind waiting."

Miss Giraffe got back her good humor and at last deliberately and very proudly, she brought out a gorgeous pair of flowery pajamas!

Everyone cried, "Ah!" and every mouth hung open with astonishment, delight, and longing.

Giving them no time to recover, Miss Giraffe—fast as a tiger's wink—pulled the pajamas on. How becoming they were! Both the top and bottom, which fitted perfectly, were covered with a pattern of flowers and leaves in yellow and red and blue, so gay, so pretty, and so different! Even the ostrich, who considered herself a style setter, could not keep from remarking in a low voice, with a hint of jealousy, "It's not bad!"

Miss Giraffe accepted every compliment with a modest air, and with her long neck extra straight, she strolled out under the bright sun.

Our Miss Giraffe enjoyed her flowery pajamas so very much that she didn't simply put them on at night, she wore them all day, morning and evening too. She kept them in the box only when it rained, for fear of spoiling them.

One morning when the sun was very hot, she decided to go swimming in the river.

She slipped out of her beautiful pajamas, hung them on a bush, and *plop!* her head was in the water. How refreshing! Her nose gleamed with drops. Miss Giraffe paddled, splashed, spluttered, even swam a little, for she was quite an athletic type. Then, having had enough diving and games, she climbed out on the bank and shook herself up and down. After that, she looked around for her pajamas. Horrors! They were gone!

The wonderful pajamas with the flowers were gone! Miss Giraffe felt close to panic. "My pajamas!" she wailed. "Where, oh, where are my pajamas?"

In just a few minutes the awful news had been heard by the whole neighborhood.

"Did you know," a chimpanzee whispered in a parrot's ear, "that the giraffe has lost her pajamas?"

The parrot swayed on his branch, gathered up all his feathers, and flew off to the gazelles, who told the ostrich, who told the zebra, who told Mrs. Chameleon—who told nobody, but looked amazed.

For a week, a long, long week, Miss Giraffe searched for her pajamas. She went over every bush and clump of green, peered into the holes where tiny creatures lived, and peered among rocks. She slid her neck inside hollow trees and pushed her nose beneath their roots. She looked at every branch and even into parrots' nests (you never know!). She even returned to the river just in case her pajamas had fallen in. She went swimming under water with her eyes open, which she didn't like, but all she saw were weeds and a few frogs quite bothered by her visit.

At the end of the week, when there was no sign of the pajamas, Miss Giraffe gave up and sadly took a walk along the border of the forest. Her spirits were so low that she hung her head down as she passed a wall of brush.

Suddenly she stopped short in surprise. Trailing out of the brush was a chameleon tail covered with a pattern of flowers and leaves in yellow and red and blue, ab-so-lute-ly like the flowers on her pajamas! With her heart thumping, she pushed her head right through the brush, and guess what she saw: lying on her pajamas—yes, her very own pajamas—were Mrs. Chameleon's five babies, entirely covered by a design of leaves and flowers!

On hearing the branches snap, Mrs. Chameleon looked up to see

Miss Giraffe and quickly exclaimed, "Aren't the little darlings beautiful like this?"

Miss Giraffe had to agree that they were beautiful with their small faces painted in four colors, and she certainly was amazed. Of course she had known for a long time that chameleons constantly change color, taking on the tone of their background. But she never would have believed the change could be as complete and perfect as this! Five chameleon babies, dressed in her pajama pattern, laughed and played; they were very glad to have a visitor.

Miss Giraffe found them all so funny that she couldn't really get cross with Mrs. Chameleon. Still, having found her pajamas again, she very much wanted to put them on, and a deep sigh rose from far down in her neck. What was she to do?

Mrs. Chameleon's face was very sad. If she had to give back the pajamas, her children would be without the pretty decorations.

Miss Giraffe thought for a long time. She adored pretty things, and she couldn't help feeling at least a little bit annoyed with Mrs. Chameleon for playing such a selfish trick; but she was also kind-hearted and extremely generous. So at last, with a big smile, she said to Mrs. Chameleon, "Look, we'll each take half. You keep the pajama top—it's big enough to make the children a nice pad—and I'll take back the bottom."

"Oh, thank you a thousand times!" cried Mrs. Chameleon, chasing her tail for joy.

Miss Giraffe went home quite pleased. She skipped along the way, and even in only half the colorful pajamas she made quite a sight!

In addition, when the neighbors learned where she had left the other half of her lovely outfit, the chimpanzees, the ostrich, the parrots, the gazelles, and the zebra all fell over each other dashing to Mrs. Chameleon's to look at the babies. And when they got there they couldn't say which they admired most, the little chameleons covered with flowers or the goodheartedness of Miss Giraffe!

THE SWING

"Hurray, hurray, hurray for the swing,"
You can hear the three shrimp children sing.

The lobster awakens from his nap,
Opens his claw with a frightful snap
And rumbling as lobsters do,
Grumbles, "Come now, off with you!"

All trembling and limp, the three little shrimp
Fumble and tumble and flee in a jumble.

THE YAK'S SHAMPOO

There were once three little mice, one white, one gray, and one black, who kept a beauty parlor.

They were wonderfully clever with their scissors, their curlers, and their combs. Customers came in droves from miles around. Some of them, such as the sheep and the egret, came very often. Others, such as the squirrel and the porcupine, dropped in only from time to time. But there was one who never came at all, absolutely never, and that was the yak. He needed attention very badly, for his coat had more tangles than a berry patch.

Imagine the surprise and delight of the three mice one Thursday afternoon when the very first customer who walked in was the yak himself, with his snarly hair.

Surprise? It was a sensation!

Still, our little mice did not forget their manners.

"Please take a seat," the white mouse invited.

Horrors!

The seat was far too small.

"Never mind!" the gray mouse and the black mouse squeaked together. In the twinkling of an eye they put all the seats they had side by side so the customer had room to sit down.

"Are you comfortable now?" the white mouse asked.

"Thank you, this is fine," the yak answered in his deep, harsh voice.

"What can we do for you?" inquired the gray mouse.

"A trim? A shampoo? Perhaps a rinse?" the black mouse suggested with her sweetest smile.

"Just a shampoo," said the yak.

It was easy to say, but what excitement it caused!

Each mouse opened a bottle of liquid shampoo and shook it onto the flowing mane. Immediately clouds, actually storms of foam rose from the yak's back. What a washday! The tiny hair-dressers, perched on the highest rung of a stepladder, rubbed and scrubbed with all their might.

Next they had to rinse away a billion bubbles. The spray in the hand basin wasn't enough; they brought in the garden hose. It was a shower bath! Water streamed from the yak's ears, but he kept his eyes half closed and never budged.

Finally, when the last bubble had disappeared, it was time for combing out. This gave the mice no trouble at all.

One behind the other they climbed the stepladder, fastened a comb in the yak's thick fleece, held tight, and *zoom!* slid all the way down to the floor. Then they climbed up again; then they slid down again. It was a good system, and besides, it was fun. They laughed and laughed.

"I'm going sledding!" cried the white mouse.

"I'm tobogganing!" cried the gray one.

"I'm an elevator!" cried the black one.

Fun though it was, the clever mice knew their job. An hour later, washed, waved, and perfumed, the yak was hard to recognize; he was very pleased with his new look.

"I'll be back next week," he promised the three mice. Then he walked out grandly past the other customers, the porcupine and the egret, who had been patiently waiting—standing—because all the seats were in use.

After such excitement, calm slowly settled in the mice's shop. Everything was put back in order, and everything went on as usual—until the next Thursday.

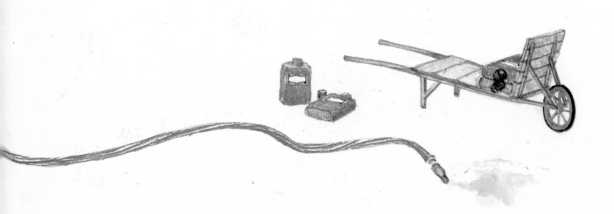

THE CALF WITH HAY FEVER

A tchoo!"

Olaf, the little calf, has hay fever.

Poor Olaf!

It's no laughing matter.

He coughs. He wheezes. His nose tickles. His throat itches. His eyes burn. His ears buzz. He sneezes and he wheezes.

Poor little calf!

All his friends make fun of him. They keep teasing, "Olaf, that's your thirty-seventh sneeze!"

A bee out on a honey hunt feels sorry for the little calf and hovers around his snout.

Olaf is terrified and starts to run.

"You big dummy!" cries the bee. "I'm not going to sting. I want to help. Stay right there and I'll come back."

Sure enough, a few minutes later, the bee flies back with a dozen friends. They are carrying a big, mysterious sack.

"There," the bee tells the calf, "we've brought a present—candy made of honey!"

"Oh, thank you!" Olaf bleats, licking up the candy. Instantly, as if by magic, he feels much better!

The bees are delighted and are very proud of their medicine. "See you tomorrow!" they promise the little calf.

And so the kind little swarm of bees takes care of Olaf with sacks of honey candy all summer long.

What a sweet way for a little calf to be cured of hay fever.

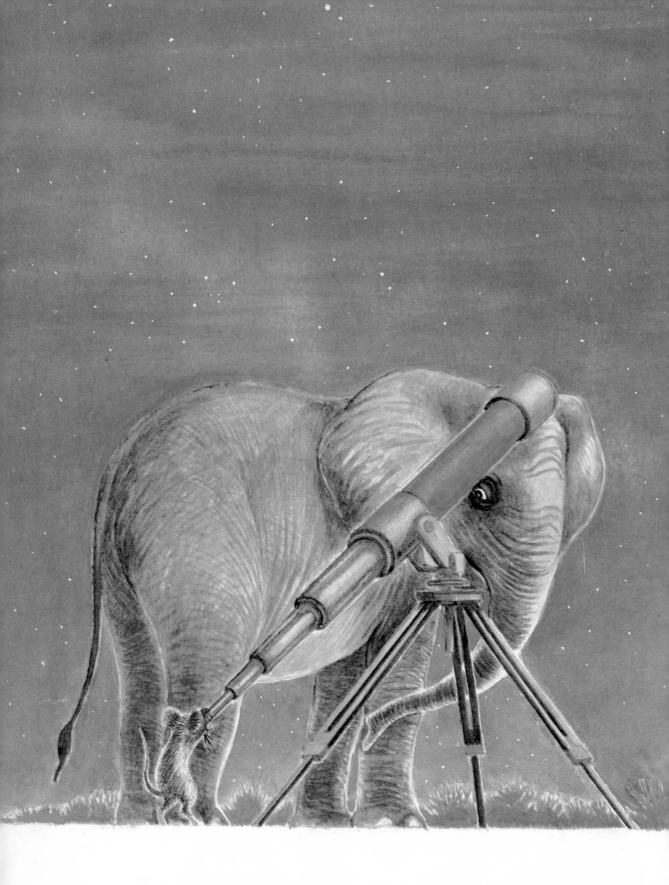

TRIP TO THE MOON

One evening when there was a full moon, Ferdinand the Elephant, and his friend Little Mouse stared up into the starry sky.

"How about going to the moon?" Little Mouse asked suddenly. Her tail began to twitch. "You know, Ferdinand, I'd like very much to take a trip. It must be so pretty up there!"

"What a wonderful idea!" cried the elephant, waving his trunk around to show that he was pleased.

Ferdinand, however, wasn't as much of a dreamer as his friend. He liked to think things out and always had to know the hows and whys. So in a little while he said again, but sadly this time, "What a wonderful idea. Only—Little Mouse, how could we ever get there? Even though you are athletic and got a gymnastics prize, you would never be able to succeed in a climb like that. You have no wings. You haven't even got a long ladder.

"As for me," he went on gloomily, "you must be making fun of me to invite me with you to the moon, because no matter how I try, I'm not able to jump higher than three apples!"

"Oh, pooh!" cried Little Mouse. "You worry too much, Ferdinand. You'll see, it can be done. Now, it's late and we must hurry to bed to be ready for the journey tomorrow."

"You mean you're really, truly thinking about going to the moon?" the elephant stammered, amazed.

"Of course," said Little Mouse simply. "And furthermore, I'm taking you along. Good night, Ferdinand, see you in the morning."

Unable to believe his big ears, the elephant mumbled, quite bewildered, "Good night, Little Mouse."

The next morning Little Mouse waltzed in to wake her friend Ferdinand while he was still snoring like a steam engine. Hop! She took him by the tail and pulled hard. This system always worked. The elephant jumped, opened an eye, and saw that she was dancing around him.

"Good morning, Ferdinand!" she cried out. "Hurry, we'll be late. Our balloons are ready to go up!"

"Our balloons?" gasped Ferdinand, still half asleep. "What balloons?"

"It would take too long to explain," said Little Mouse, wriggling impatiently. "Come along."

Meekly, the elephant clumped away behind his friend.

"There you are!" Little Mouse announced triumphantly pointing to a pair of very odd flying machines in a clearing. Ferdinand's eyes bulged. There, floating in front of him, were two balloons, a blue one and a yellow one, each fastened by a dozen cords to a wicker basket—a small basket and a big one. Before Ferdinand could have said "abracadabra," his friend had hopped into the small basket and had begun throwing out the rocks that kept it down.

"I did it all myself," she boasted, tossing the last pebble out. "And as you can imagine—"

But suddenly, *zoom!* without the extra weight, Little Mouse's basket, pulled by the balloon, started off for space!

"Wait for me!" cried Ferdinand, and just in the nick of time he caught the basket with the very tip of his trunk.

Not bothered at all by taking off so fast, Little Mouse beamed. "It works!" she squeaked. "You can see it works! In a quarter of an hour we'll be on the moon!"

Ferdinand began to feel more hopeful in spite of himself. First, he quickly fastened Little Mouse's balloon to his so they wouldn't be blown away from each other up there in the clouds. Then, with a big grin, he settled in his basket. One by one he dropped out the stones that—he supposed—were holding his balloon on the ground. After chucking the last one into the grass, he closed his eyes and waited to soar.

Alas, he didn't move even an inch. Not a thing happened! All his hopes were over in a flash. "I knew it," he groaned. "I knew I weighed too much to go up to the moon." Two large tears trickled down his trunk.

Little Mouse was very cross. "No, you don't weigh too much to go to the moon," she snapped, "but you're too stupid! Come on—if your basket won't go up with one balloon, we'll get ten, that's all! Dry your tears and come with me."

Ferdinand, ashamed, obeyed her without any questions. Rather to the elephant's surprise, his friend led the way to a shoe store where the owner, a smart, conceited baboon, was giving away balloons as prizes to anyone who bought his shoes. As Ferdinand understood why they had gone there, he was lost in admiration of Little Mouse's cleverness.

"Please, Mr. Baboon, could we have ten balloons?" Little Mouse asked.

"Ten balloons! That's quite a lot," the monkey answered, scratch-

ing his head. "You would have to do something for me in return."

Little Mouse, who never seemed to run out of ideas, offered to clean the store. The baboon was willing, and the bargain was made. So all day long Little Mouse, with a duster in her paws, chased after dust and fluff, while Ferdinand, with a pail of water and rags, washed and polished every window in the store, making fine use of .his trunk. When night came the two friends had earned their ten balloons.

Yet in spite of the added number and the gay colors, ten balloons were not enough to lift the elephant. Ferdinand was absolutely crushed. "It's impossible," he said. "Little Mouse, you must go to the moon without me!"

"Out of the question!" replied Little Mouse, swishing her tail.

"If your basket won't go up with ten balloons, we'll get a hundred. It's perfectly simple!"

The baboon, on the other hand, was not so sure. "One hundred balloons," he chattered, raising his paws, "one hundred balloons! What on earth will you do with a hundred balloons?"

"Go to the moon," said Little Mouse calmly.

"Oho!" said the baboon, "you won't fool an old monkey like me with a story like that. Just the same, if you work in the store for a week, I'll give you a hundred balloons."

So for a whole week Ferdinand and his friend Little Mouse swept out, scrubbed, and tidied up Mr. Baboon's store. On the last evening he gave them a hundred balloons and sarcastically wished them a good trip.

Ferdinand and Little Mouse had to go back and forth thirty-six times to carry all those balloons and fasten them to the baskets.

At last it was done. Our two adventurers were all ready to leave. From Little Mouse's basket floated one lone yellow balloon, and from the elephant's, bobbing and rubbing together, a hundred in all colors.

At the very same instant, Little Mouse and Ferdinand threw out their last bit of ballast, and at the very same instant the two baskets sprang up toward the sky! Little Mouse clapped with all four feet, while Ferdinand, almost too excited to speak, got out, "I'm flying! I'm flying! I feel light as a bird! Oh, it's beautiful! This is the best day of my life!"

However, if Ferdinand thought he was like a bird, the birds thought they had lost their minds when they saw a big elephant drifting past. Terrified, they flew away as fast as they could. Ferdinand and Little Mouse burst out laughing. Then they noticed three chimpanzees in the branches of a baobab. They called out, "Good morning! How are you?" surprising the monkeys so that they fell over backward. Then our two friends gathered some nice ripe fruit from the top of a banana tree. "Here's our food for the trip!" cried Little Mouse, very pleased. Caught in a sudden air current, they were whisked away and found themselves a lot higher, up among the clouds.

"Hurray! Hurray! We're getting to the moon!" sang Little Mouse, jumping up and down in her basket so hard that she nearly fell out. Ankles crossed, ears fluttering, Ferdinand wore his most angelic smile.

Then the wind began to swirl around the two flying machines. Further on, the sky looked very dark.

"Hang on!" Little Mouse called to the elephant. "It's nothing but a squall!"

Hunched down inside their baskets, clinging tightly to the cords, the adventurers felt themselves tossed in all directions by a wind that grew stronger and stronger. At last, with a roar, a tornado struck—they were in the center of it! Thunder crashed; lightning flashed. Little Mouse, brave as she was, began to shake with fright. As for poor Ferdinand, who was clutching at his hundred balloons with his trunk, he expected to tumble out into space at any moment.

Tick! tack! A shower of hailstones hit the travelers, and their balloons began to burst. The storm never let up for an instant. As the last balloons popped, the baskets and their passengers were tum-

bling at top speed toward the ground. *Boom!* Ferdinand and Little Mouse, half-stunned, found themselves in the middle of a turnip field.

"Are you all right?" asked an odd-looking person with long ears.

It was Mr. Hare. He had been smoking a pipe by his front door when to his astonishment he had seen Ferdinand and Little Mouse fall out of the sky into his garden. Being very polite, he didn't ask any questions and thought only of what help he could offer the two strangers.

"Nothing broken?" he went on cheerfully. "My name is Mr. Hare.

Come inside and have a bowl of soup to warm you up."

Our friends accepted his invitation, and five minutes later all their troubles were forgotten in front of a handsome soup tureen.

"What delicious stew!" cried Little Mouse, taking another helping. "What is it?"

"Turnip soup, neither more nor less," answered Mr. Hare.

Little Mouse wrinkled up her forehead, thought hard, and went on eating silently. But when it came time to leave, after thanking

Mr. Hare for his hospitality, she asked in her sweetest voice, "Please, Mr. Hare, could you spare us a few turnips?"

"Very easily," said the hare. "As you can see, I have a field full."

"Oh, thank you! thank you! What a wonderful gift," said Little Mouse. "Good-by, Mr. Hare, and maybe we'll see you again soon."

"It would be a pleasure," answered the hare, waving good-by with his ears.

Carrying the turnip sack, Little Mouse climbed on Ferdinand's back, and he trudged into the forest. Because he was on solid ground, and most of all because he had had a lot to eat, the elephant felt brave again.

At a turn of the path the moon came suddenly in view. "Ah," sighed Little Mouse, looking sad, "we'll have to go there some other time. But at least we had a lot of fun today, Ferdinand, didn't we?"

"Oh, yes," Ferdinand agreed, happy that it was all over. "By the way, what are you going to do with all these turnips? Make soup? It's a fine idea!"

"No, no," said Little Mouse. "It's a secret—you will see."

It took our two travelers all that night to get back to their home town. As soon as they arrived, instead of going to bed, Little Mouse hurried off with Ferdinand to the baboon's shoe store.

"Here we are back from the moon!" she boasted. "We had a splendid time!"

The baboon made a face to show that he couldn't be fooled and didn't believe a word of it.

Not disturbed at all, as Ferdinand stood absolutely lost in admiration, Little Mouse went right on, "We thought of you up there, Mr. Baboon. We picked moon vegetables, and we have brought you some!"

Thump! Little Mouse dropped the sack of Mr. Hare's turnips onto the counter.

The baboon was so surprised at the sight of these vegetables, which he had never seen before, that he couldn't tell what to believe. He

who had always teased everybody else, played a thousand tricks, and had been a master at pranks and fibs risked being fooled for the first time in his life! He couldn't be sure what was true and what was false: whether Little Mouse was joking or quite serious. He felt silly. What could he say? He rolled his eyes, opened and shut his mouth a dozen times as if he were trying to catch flies, made a face, pawed the air, cleared his throat, and finally got out, "Thanks." Then he kept still.

The sight of his predicament was so funny that Ferdinand said afterward it was well worth a "trip to the moon."

THE ZEBRA WITH CHECKS

An absent-minded zebra sat down on a bench one
day, not noticing the sign that said "Fresh Paint."
And this is how he looked when he got up.

TINY TURTLE'S SORE THROAT

Tiny Turtle woke up one morning with a terribly sore throat. It tickled; it itched; it stung!

"Oh, ouch, I can't swallow!" the poor sufferer exclaimed, and instead of going out into the garden to play, he didn't move from the rug where he slept.

His mother brought his breakfast, hot cocoa steaming in a little cup with flowers, and good-smelling buttered toast.

"Good morning," said Mother Turtle cheerfully. "Still in bed, lazy bones?"

"Good morning," said Tiny Turtle, making a face because it hurt

to talk. "Mama," he whined, "my throat is on fire. I feel as if I had swallowed one million mosquitoes!"

"Try to drink your cocoa anyway," his mother said.

Tiny Turtle took the pretty cup but couldn't get a mouthful down. "Mama!" he cried, "there is a great big cactus stuck in my throat! Really there is!"

"That's a little hard to believe," Mother Turtle smiled. "More likely you have caught a chill. I'll call up the doctor."

She telephoned Dr. Parrot, and fifteen minutes later there he was by Tiny Turtle's bed, with his bag under his wing.

All he could see of Tiny Turtle was a big round shell.

"Hello," he began, in his sharp voice. "Let's have a look at that throat, Tiny Turtle. Then we'll cure you right away."

Hidden tight inside his shell, Tiny Turtle never stirred. Feet, nose—nothing peeped out.

"Here, here," muttered Dr. Parrot, not knowing where to start with this lump of shell. He couldn't even tell which was head and which was tail.

He walked all the way around, rather puzzled, while Mother Turtle, who was upset, kept repeating, "You bad child, come out this minute!"

Tiny Turtle stayed quite still.

Dr. Parrot, who was very patient with patients, took a flashlight from his bag, lay down flat beside the sickbed, and began crawling around with the light turned on the patient. He hoped to make Tiny Turtle so curious that he would just have to come out of his shell. As a matter of fact, Tiny Turtle very much wanted to see the interesting light up close, but he had promised himself to stay hidden.

"Well, there's nothing I can do!" decided Dr. Parrot, getting up again. "Good-by, Mrs. Turtle, I'll be back when your youngster feels in a better mood. Don't you worry, though," he went on, "It

looks like nothing but a sore throat. In that case the cure is easy. You know it just as well as I do—some sweet syrup, and especially ice cream, lots and lots of ice cream. That's the very best thing for—"

He hadn't finished speaking before Tiny Turtle came out of his shell like magic, moving as fast as his little legs could go, and opened his mouth wide, simply begging for his throat to be looked at. "I'm sure it's a sore throat!" he cried. "I can tell. You'll see. I need lots and lots and lots of ice cream!"

Dr. Parrot smiled, gave a wink to Mother Turtle, opened his bag, put on his round head-lamp, took a spoon, and ordered Tiny Turtle to say "Ah."

"Ah! Ah! Ah!" Tiny Turtle cried joyfully.

"Yes, a little inflammation," said Dr. Parrot, "nothing to feel alarmed about." Then he frowned and gave his young patient a severe look.

"You really didn't need to make that big a fuss, you little rascal."

Tiny Turtle was ashamed, hung his head, and promised never to behave like that again.

"Well, I forgive you," the doctor went on in a kinder tone, "because, you see, I have learned something. To bring you out of your shell, I need only say the magic words 'ice cream!' I'll remember from now on. Good-by, Tiny Turtle, and take care of yourself."

Dr. Parrot left, his bag under his wing.

While Mother Turtle was fetching the syrup and the ice cream, Tiny Turtle tucked himself back inside his shell and fell fast asleep, smiling happily.

THE DRESSED-UP DOLPHIN

Shimmering brightly from tail to fin,
His costume dotted, knotted, and strung
With sea urchins, seaweed, starfish, and hung

With coral, pearls, and the fanciest shells,
Which swing as he sways, and chink-tinkle like bells,
The outlandishly droll, whimsical dolphin
Goes off to the ball as Harlequin!
Clashing his conch-shell cymbals,
Into the grand hall he glides,
Amidst Oh! and Ah! from all sides:
Oh, look, look at him!
Why, it's Harlequin—
That outlandishly droll, whimsical dolphin!

THE OSTRICH WHO LOVED PAINTINGS

Once upon a time there was an ostrich who loved paintings—not painting them herself, but visiting galleries, shops, or museums just to look at them.

She wasn't difficult to please. She liked painted faces just as much as painted flowers, and painted country scenes just as much as plain designs. Anything at all that had been painted

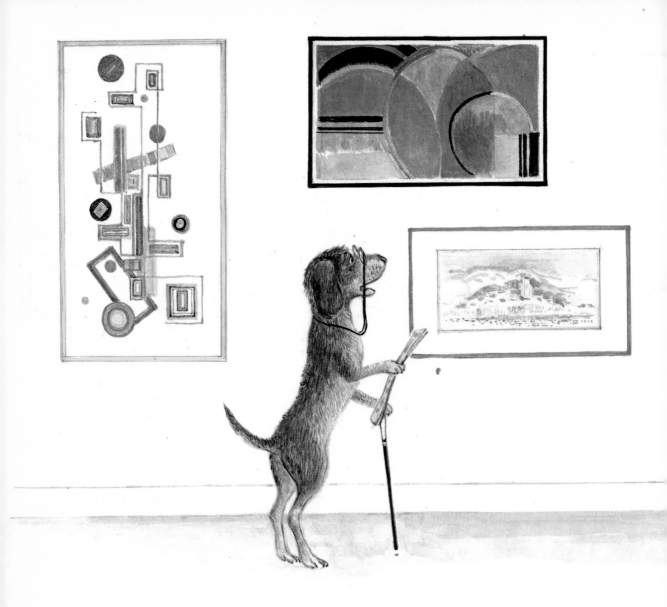

amused her—squiggles or straight lines, the wildest colors or the mildest ones.

This ostrich actually was a bit featherbrained and very easily excited—really much too easily, for every time she went to look at pictures she had an accident. Every single time!

For example, yesterday, Wednesday, she went out early to Rose Flamingo's gallery, where some new paintings had been hung. Well, she had hardly set foot inside the door before she was gasping and

flapping, whirling left and right and round and round, and squawking with all her might!

The paintings were in every color, size, and shape. The ostrich was quite carried away. She stooped and twisted with her long neck and ran up and down the gallery as if she needed to gape at everything at the same time. She looked as if she were on a turntable. Just watching her made Rose Flamingo very dizzy.

"My dear ostrich, do keep still for a minute!" Miss Flamingo begged.

Surprised, the ostrich paused, then dashed away again.

"You ought to have a dozen eyes!" a dapper old dog teased good-naturedly.

"Yes, of course I ought," the ostrich answered seriously, spinning like a top.

By the end of the morning the thing that always occurred when our ostrich looked at pictures had happened—she had gotten her neck into such knots and her head so back to front that whether she liked it or not, she had to walk home backward! After that she had to send for the doctor as quickly as she could.

He was a parrot with a great deal of patience. He had treated her before.

"Here you are again with your head wrong side around," he scolded through his feathers. "You know it isn't sensible. Oh, well, let's get on with the cure. Turn your head a little to the right. Good. Now, to the left. Good. Right, left. Right, left. . . ."

For half an hour Dr. Parrot, quiet and calm, helped the ostrich untie her neck. "That's done," he said at last. "Now get some rest and don't let it happen again."

"No, I certainly won't!" clucked the ostrich, for her head ached terribly.

She put on an ice bag and stretched out on the sofa with her eyes nearly closed.

You'd never believe it, but all those aches and pains didn't keep our featherbrain from starting all over again the very next day, tangling her skinny neck in knots! This time it was from looking at flower pictures.

One of these days she'll lose her head over a painting. . . .

KITCHEN GARDEN CONCERT

Little hedgehog Leo
Scrambles to a pumpkin top
And looks out on the garden crop.
Unfolding his accordion,
He plays a mischievous charleston.

"Bravo, Leo, Bravo!"
Three dizzy dancing linnets cry,
As under the carrots they whirl on by.

Bouncing through the radish crop,
Four field mice cheer and tease:
"More, let's have some more, Leo, please!"

Beaming proudly from the pumpkin top
The little hedgehog does not stop;
On he plays, as round they prance:
"Please, Leo, just one more dance!"

THE UPS AND DOWNS OF THE
HERON WHO WAS DYING TO SKI

One day a rooster and a heron set out together for winter sports. They were both dying to ski.

As soon as they arrived, they got their equipment and signed up for lessons with the well-known teacher, Mr. Bear.

The rooster showed real talent right away. You ought to have seen him on the slopes, with his comb and tail feathers flying in the breeze! All the other skiers stopped to admire him and cheer.

The heron, on the other hand, couldn't ski at all. He fell down once a minute, and when he wasn't actually falling he still looked as if he were bound to break his neck or his leg. He had a whole string of accidents. Once he landed beak down in a drift and was stuck fast, twisted halfway around and half smothered too, till the teacher came and tugged him out.

Soon afterward he went smack into a tree and saw two dozen stars!

Then, with no warning, he slid backward and landed *flop!* on his back with both legs up!

Sometimes he strayed off course, though he had tried hard to follow the track marked by Mr. Bear, and tore down the awful slope in a storm of snow, ending up wrapped tight into a snowball at the bottom!

And yet no matter what happened to him, the heron wouldn't give up. Mr. Bear had to admire such a brave and stubborn pupil, and he longed to discover some way he could help.

One day he had a wonderful idea! "I know why you have so

much trouble!" he told the heron. "It's your beak—that long, long beak. It throws you off balance. Your beak has got to have a ski!"

It was no sooner said than done. The heron was given a third ski, and at once, magically, his problems were at an end!

Now he could fly down the steepest slopes like a rocket and never

tumble at all. Mr. Bear had guessed exactly right! With a ski attached to the tip of his beak, the heron became a ski champion in a very few days, and when the great downhill race was held for the finest skiers, he got first place! His friend the rooster had to be content to come in second.

THE GREEDY LITTLE BROWN COW

There was once a little brown cow who lived on a farm at the foot of a mountain.

This little cow had a fine disposition. She was always ready to laugh and make jokes, and she never failed to say something nice to anyone who came along, to the mole as well as to the donkey, and even to Gruffy the Hedgehog.

But, alas, the little cow had one serious fault. She was very, very greedy. The grass in her field, tasty as it was, didn't satisfy her. She wanted something more, something extra, tidbits. To be frank, what she wanted was the wonderful flowers growing on the tiptop of the mountain.

This little cow was a good climber, so every afternoon she bravely scampered up the rocks and ledges to the summit. Once she got there, what a treat! First she drank in all the warm sweet odors brought by a little breeze. Then she lay down on the grass and with her eyes shining cropped up all the flowers she could reach, happily munching the velvet petals, the crisp stems, and the tangy, juicy leaves. It was a real feast. She chewed up daisies and buttercups, clover and dandelions, by the bunch. Most of all, though—yes, most of all—the blue, blue periwinkles were her favorites.

Finally she would stop, thinking sensibly, "I must leave something for tomorrow." She would get ready to climb down the mountainside.

Misery!

That was where her troubles always began.

Though climbing up was very easy, going down was horrible. The sight of such a drop made her dizzy. She had to look away, and sometimes shut her eyes altogether. Not watching where she put her hoofs, she would stumble, bang her shins, and sometimes lose her balance completely, rolling over and over to the edge of a cliff!

It was like a nightmare.

When at last she reached the farm she was always so tired, with so many aches and pains, that she could hardly drag herself to her stall and flop down on the straw.

"This won't do at all," her friend the magpie said one day.

"Not at all!" agreed her other friend, the farmyard dog. "You'll either break your neck or wear yourself out until you're ill."

"I know," the little brown cow agreed sadly, "but whatever will become of me if I can't get my precious little flowers?"

"Don't feel upset," croaked the magpie. "I have an idea."

Hop! the magpie perched herself on the cow's head and whispered a plan into one ear. The dog moved close so as not to miss a single word. When the magpie had finished, both the cow and the dog stared

at her, their eyes glistening with admiration, and said from the bottom of their hearts, "How marvelous!"

Then, with mysterious expressions on their faces, the three friends parted. The dog went to his kennel by the farmyard gate, the magpie to her roost up in the pine—and as for the cow she curled up in the warm straw and fell fast asleep.

The magpie woke bright and early the next morning. She chose a spot high in her tree and kept watch, not stirring even a feather. From there, at last she saw the farmer's wife cross the yard lugging a basket. She stopped at the clothesline, set the basket down, and filled it with the sheets and towels that had dried. Then she picked up the basket again and walked away.

"Here we go!" the magpie told herself. *Zoom!* she flew for the yard, settled on a clothesline post, and *tick-tack*, with the tip of her beak she undid one end of the line. Then she flew to the other post and *tick-tack*, she undid the other end. Then, the line held firmly in her beak, she headed at top speed to the barn, while the line turned and twisted behind her in a thousand loops.

In the meantime, at the kennel, eyes squinting and ears pricked, the dog waited for the farmer to start work as he did every morning in the nearby field. The moment this happened, he leaped to his paws and raced inside the farmhouse. Skidding around a cupboard,

he spread his jaws wide and seized the old mended umbrella that the farmer kept in the corner with his boots. Then he set off again madly, but somehow he couldn't get through the door and had to make three tries before he realized that with an umbrella in his mouth he had to go out sideways. Finally he succeeded, shot across the yard without a glance at the rooster crowing on the henhouse, and dashed into the barn.

What went on inside the barn you'll soon find out.

An hour later the magpie came out and flew up to her pine. The dog trotted to his kennel. Last of all, the little brown cow made her appearance.

Warned by the rooster, all the henhouse creatures crowded to the fence so as not to miss a thing.

"What has she got on?" a turkey squawked.

"Look at that get-up!" clucked the hens.

"You would think it were Halloween," cackled an old goose who always rattled out anything that came into his head.

This time he wasn't far wrong, for the little cow did seem to be dressed in a most peculiar way. She wore the clothesline wrapped around her half a dozen times. From her waist hung an extra length of cord—the magpie must have worn down her beak doing so many knots!—and from this cord hung the mended, faded umbrella, half opened.

However, the little cow trik-trotted down the fence as if this outfit were quite usual, and because she was so good-natured she gave

everyone her nicest smile—the rooster, the turkeys, the pullets, the geese, the hens, and even every small chick. After that she started gaily up the mountain path, seeming not to be bothered by the dangling umbrella that bounced behind her from rock to rock.

Birds seesawing in a fir tree watched with popping eyes. "Yoo-hoo, friend cow," they twittered. "It's so sunny today; why are you taking an umbrella?"

"You'll know this afternoon," the little cow answered. She gave them a wink and continued on her way.

One last hump, one last bank! With a heave, the little brown cow had reached the summit. She relaxed on some moss to enjoy a thousand and one delicious buds. They had never tasted so good. "What a feast!" mooed the little cow, bobbing her head from side to side in her enjoyment.

Then it was time to go down. Very carefully she went over in her mind what the magpie had told her to do. After walking to the very edge of the cliff, she turned her head away—because honestly all that space did make her dizzy—closed her eyes tight, took a big breath, and gathering all her strength, jumped right out with her hoofs together!

Instantly the umbrella opened and proved to be a splendid parachute. Before she could say, "One, two, three!" there she was swinging at the end of her cord, gently drifting toward the farm.

"It's impossible," she mumbled. "It must be a dream." She risked opening one eye. What she saw was indeed dreamlike—the whole countryside lay there below—but as she no longer felt that she would fall or lose her balance, she was not a bit afraid. So she opened her other eye and with both eyes wide stared at her farm, her field, and her barn, which were slowly drawing near.

Without any effort or alarm she continued to move down. "It's a dream," she said again as she floated on a tiny breeze. "The magpie certainly is smart!"

Just then some butterflies fluttering around were almost knocked to bits by her hoofs. They scattered in a rush, wing over wing. "A cow in the sky!" they exclaimed. "It can't be true!" They were so surprised that they almost forgot to fly and fell dizzily downward. But once the first shock was over, they came close and danced in a wreath around her horns. Smiling, the cow called, "Peekaboo," and drifted on down.

Below, it was the rooster who spotted her first. At once he sounded an alert, and the farm creatures turned their eyes to the

sky. They made such a racket that the farmer and his wife ran out
to look. They found the poultry in a circle in the yard, necks
stretched towards the clouds, screeching as loudly as they could.
In the center the dog jumped up and down and barked, with the
magpie perched between his ears. Mr. Mole was there too, and the
donkey, and Gruffy the Hedgehog.

Wondering what it was all about, the farmer and his wife lifted
their eyes too, and, like the poultry, the magpie, the dog, Mr. Mole,
the donkey, and Gruffy the Hedgehog, they saw swinging to the left,

then swinging to the right, twirling without a trace of fear under that old umbrella and even laughing so she showed every tooth—none other than their own little brown cow!

"My, oh, my!" exclaimed the farmer's wife, rubbing her eyes.

The farmer couldn't help bursting out, "So, that's where my umbrella went!"

Little by little they got over their surprise and began to laugh.

Just a few minutes later the little cow made a safe landing in the yard. "It was a perfect trip," she said at once, smiling at all those who welcomed her. "I feel fine." With a glance at the dog and the magpie, instead of clumping to the barn, she pranced off to her field in the best of spirits and started to browse. She left the equipment on her back to be used the next day.

The other farm creatures had a harder time settling down. The whole yard was filled with cackling, crowing, and clucking until far into the night.

Mr. Mole went home quite dazzled by all he had seen. Gruffy the Hedgehog forgot to be gruff for several hours. The donkey mumbled something about wishing *he* had a parachute to help him down to the village with his cart. It was quite a while before he got this hopeless thought out of his head.

What about the magpie and the dog?

They acted as if they had lost their minds, racing around the field, flying and galloping, while the little brown cow grazed.

"Hooray! Hooray!" they shrieked. "We did it!"

Standing beside his wife, the farmer scratched his head and sighed, thinking things out. He was truly fond of his little cow. "As a matter of fact," he reminded himself, "I would hate to have her break a leg. If she's found a safe way to get down the mountain, it's all to the good." Then he said aloud to his wife, "I suppose all I can do is buy myself a new umbrella."

"And I'll buy myself another clothesline," said his wife. Then they began to laugh some more, very pleased to have agreed.

Ever since that day the little brown cow has led a perfectly happy life. She is known far and wide as That Cow with the Umbrella.

MIC-MAC

Oh, what bad luck!
Mic-Mac the duck
Has got the mumps.
He cannot quack;
His cheeks are lumps!

Now Mother Duck has tucked him in
A hammock. "Be my brave birdling,"
She says, "and take your medicine;
You will get better while you swing,
Your cheeks will soon grow nice and thin,
And how you'll quack, and quack,
Mic-Mac!"

THE CROCODILE'S CONCERT

One evening the crocodile decided to give a concert.

Looking proud and pleased with himself, he slithered up on the platform, and with many waves and bows to the audience, picked up his saxophone. He faced front, drew a tremendous breath, puffed out his cheeks, and blew as fiercely as he could.

He blew into the saxophone, but not a sound came out!

The crocodile, amazed, had no idea what could be wrong: he kept calm, and blew again, twice as hard. His cheeks seemed ready to burst! He turned red, his scales rose up on end, and his tail stood straight above his head!

But there still was not the smallest sound.

Even worse, the audience began to laugh. Everyone laughed very hard—and harder, and harder!

You may have figured out already why they had laughed, but the crocodile still couldn't guess what was causing the silence in the saxophone and the uproar in the audience.

Angrily he yanked the saxophone around, and so at last he found what everybody else had known for several minutes—that the desert fox was taking a nap curled up cozily right inside the opening. Right inside his saxophone!

The crocodile reared back. He hunched, he stretched, he scowled, he rewrinkled every wrinkle. He flashed lightning from his eyes and clashed his scales.

Everyone laughed twice as hard.

As the racket grew, the desert fox—luckily—woke up, jumped from the saxophone, and rushed away, not stopping to ask questions.

Shaking with rage, the crocodile stamped, swayed, exclaimed, complained, threw down the saxophone, and left the platform.

The concert was over. The listeners hadn't heard a single note of music, but how they had laughed!

Funny concert, don't you think?

FOLLOW THE LEADER

One morning a gnat left the violet he was using as a home and started for a walk, hop, hop, through the big meadow.

Now an ant noticed the gnat and said to herself, "Aha! Let's follow this little creature; it would make a nice mouthful!"

A June bug noticed the ant and said to herself, "Aha! Let's follow this attractive ant; it would make a nice mouthful!"

A field mouse noticed the June bug and said to himself, "Aha! Let's follow this fat June bug; it would make a nice mouthful!"

A weasel noticed the field mouse and said to herself, "Aha! Let's follow this lovely field mouse; it would make a nice mouthful!"

A fox noticed the weasel and said to himself, "Aha! Let's follow this plump weasel; it would make a nice mouthful!"

A bear noticed the fox and said to himself, "Aha! Let's follow this tempting fox; it would make a nice mouthful!"

In this way, following the leader, bear, fox, weasel, field mouse, June bug, ant, and gnat went walking one behind the other all around the meadow!

By and by the gnat began to feel just the least little bit uneasy.

It seemed as if there might be somebody following!

So he turned.

And there was the ant, all ready to gobble him up!

Quickly, at the top of his lungs, he shouted, "Hey, ant, look around!"

The ant turned and saw the June bug all ready to gobble her up.

Quickly, at the top of her lungs, she shouted, "Hey, June bug, look around!"

The June bug turned, and there was the field mouse, all ready to gobble her up. Quickly, at the top of her lungs, she shouted, "Hey, field mouse, look behind!"

The field mouse turned, and there was the weasel, all ready to gobble him up. Quickly, at the top of his lungs, he shouted, "Hey, weasel, look around!"

The weasel turned and there was the fox, all ready to gobble her

up. Quickly, at the top of her lungs, she shouted, "Hey, fox, look around!"

The fox turned, and there was the bear, all ready to gobble him up. He too, like the gnat, the ant, the June bug, the field mouse, and the weasel, shouted at the top of his lungs, "Hey, bear, look around!"

The bear turned—and saw nothing at all!

But meanwhile the fox, along with the others, had made a run for it.

Yes, in no time the gnat, ant, June bug, field mouse, weasel, and fox had scattered to the four corners of the meadow, scampered into their homes, and shut themselves up tight.

The bear, furious at having been tricked, went to sulk inside his den.

For the rest of the day nobody showed so much as a whisker anywhere.

THE LINNET

Look where that foolish linnet has made her nest! It's a good thing the stag is very patient.

He has promised to wait until the baby birds know how to fly before shaking off his annoying hat.

He is certainly very kind, for the nest is not convenient for him—he has to hold his head up while he sleeps and walk step by step so as not to spill his load of tiny birds.

No wonder he reminds the linnet every day, "Another time, think it over; don't confuse my antlers with the branches of some tree!"

But next year, you just wait and see. . . .

RATATAM'S BATHTUB

Once upon a time there was a hippopotamus named Ratatam. He was a strange character. He never did anything quite like any other hippopotamus, and his head was always full of odd ideas.

That is why one fine morning Ratatam decided he must put a bathtub in his hut.

Yes, indeed, a bathtub! "—because I've had quite enough," our peculiar hippopotamus said to anyone who happened by, "absolutely enough, of bathing in the river! The water is cold and dirty, and

worst of all, you get your feet caught in those sticky water weeds!"

Ratatam's friends shook their heads, laughed behind his back, and decided they would wait and see.

Answering an emergency call, the plumber arrived and quickly took out his tools and made measurements. Then he scratched his chin, screwed up his baboon eyes, and said, "Mr. Ratatam, I'm not sure I can get a bathtub big enough."

"Never mind! It doesn't matter. I must have a bathtub!" cried the hippopotamus, who was very set in his ideas but had very little practical sense and no patience.

"All right, all right," the plumber said.

Three days later he delivered the most marvelous blue bathtub with shiny faucets.

Our Ratatam could hardly wait to take a bath. Grinning from ear to ear, he turned the faucets on, letting in the hot and cold water and sighing with delight as the water splashed and the tub filled. When it was quite full he clambered over the edge and *plop!* he sat down like a king.

But—but what was happening?

In less than a second the bathtub was empty and a pool of water covered the floor of the hut.

"Oh, oh!" rumbled the hippopotamus, worried and annoyed. "What does this mean?"

He climbed out of the bathtub, drew another bath, and for the second time got into the water. As if by magic, in the twinkling of an eye the tub was empty while the flood in the hut rose twice as high.

Now he was really angry. "That plumber!" he cried. "What a rascal! He has sold me a leaky tub!"

He rushed to the telephone and ordered the plumber to come right away.

The baboon jumped on his bicycle and arrived to find the hippopotamus red and yellow and green with rage, stuttering, hiccuping, threatening, stamping, and calling him a dozen names. "You nitwit! You good-for-nothing! You cheat!"

"But what on earth is the matter?" cried the plumber.

"What's the matter?" roared back the hippopotamus. "You ask me what's the matter? Well, the matter is, you robber, you villain, that you sold me a leaky tub. Do you hear? My bathtub has holes!"

"That would surprise me very much," said the baboon, remaining calm. At that Ratatam nearly choked with rage, and only after jumping up and down till he was almost out of breath would he explain his two misfortunes to the plumber.

With a slight smile, the plumber pointed out, "I did warn you, Mr. Ratatam, that this model isn't big enough. Or to put it another way, you are too big for your tub, and so it overflows. There's room for the water, or there's room for you, but not for both. Together, you add up to a catastrophe. You are just too big."

"Too big!" cried the hippopotamus, as if he couldn't believe his

ears. "Too big, you say! Oh, this is just too much! You oaf, I am going to teach you some manners!"

Boom! Ratatam threw himself at the baboon. The baboon, however, twisted free, jumped back on his bicycle, and was gone in three whirls of the pedals. Ratatam ran after him, but it was no use—the plumber was already far away, and the poor hippopotamus could only pant.

He turned back and went inside his hut, head down. But the sight of the blue bathtub, leaky or not, made him furious again. And shoving with his shoulders and feet, Ratatam got the dreadful object out of the house. He kicked and pushed it across the grass to the river and finally, with all his strength, he heaved it deep into the water!

Amazingly enough, the bathtub, after jouncing several times, began to float! It drifted peacefully along the current.

Ratatam jumped for joy on the bank, dived in, swam a stroke or two, hauled himself into the queer boat, and settled down with a huge smile. Then he let himself rock gently on the tide, and whenever he got too hot he had only to dip a foot over the side and give himself a splash or a whole shower and sail on again, humming, "A floating bathtub, in the open air—how heavenly, a dream!"

His friends, the other hippopotamuses, were astonished. They said to one another huffily, "Just another crazy idea!" But secretly they really envied that comfortable modern arrangement.

As for the baboon, no one is supposed to know that hidden by the leaves of the baobab tree, he is taking a photograph of his unusual customer drifting in the tub in the middle of the river. He will hang it on the window of his shop as an advertisement, and he'll probably become famous.